BE HAPPY

SANGEETA SHARMA

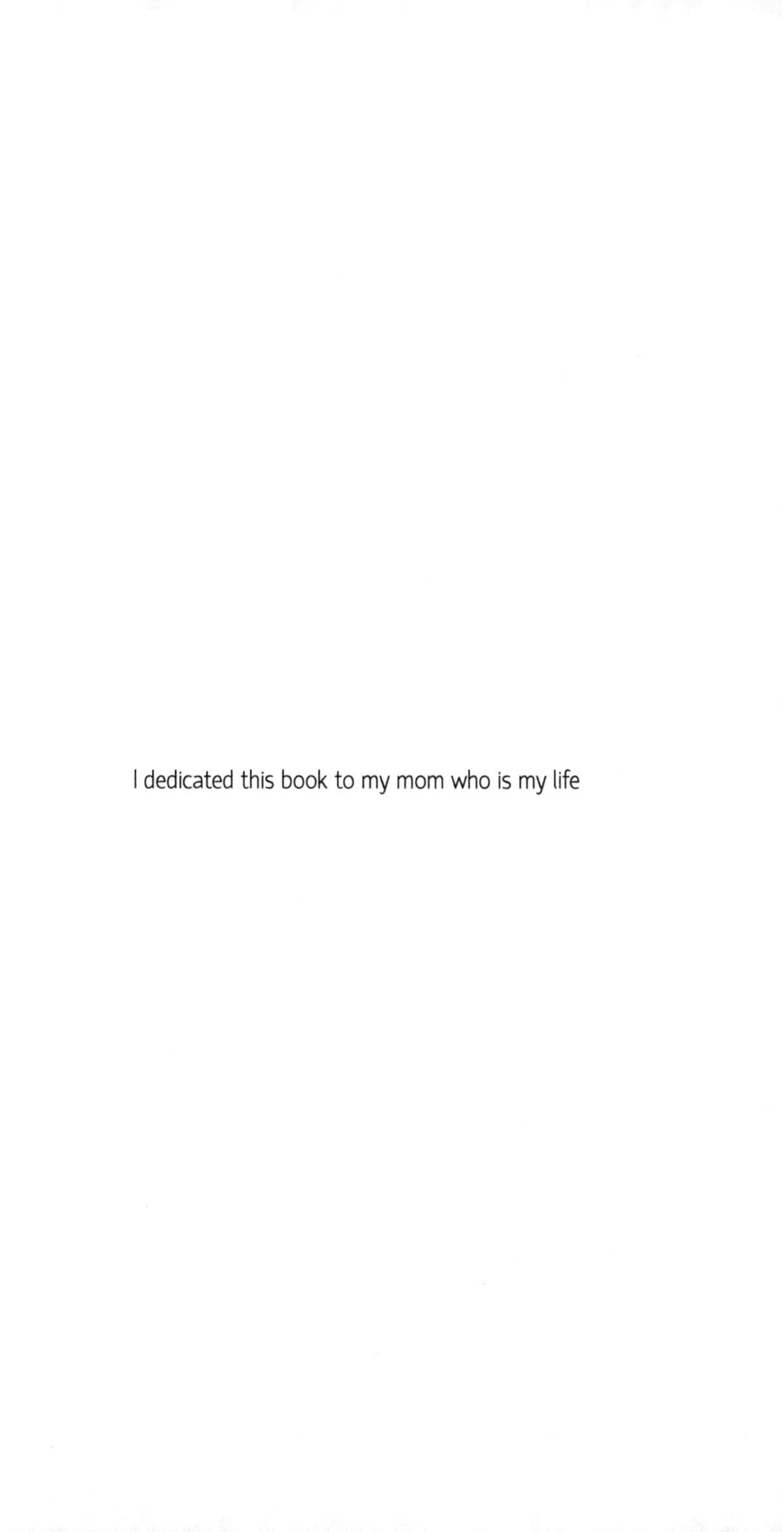

I dedicated this book to my mom who is my life

Contents

Foreword

thanks for your support

Preface

BE happy

Acknowledgements

Get rEady

Prologue

I know wha happen but i know what not happend

CHAPTER ONE

Good mental

As of 2016, no evidence of happiness causing improved physical health has been found; the topic is being researched at the Lee Kum Sheung Center for Health and Happiness at the Harvard T.H. Chan School of Public Health.[118] A positive relationship has been suggested between the volume of the brain's gray matter in the right precuneus area and one's subjective happiness score.[119]

Sonja Lyubomirsky has estimated that 50 percent of a given human's happiness level could be genetically determined, 10 percent is affected by life circumstances and situation, and a remaining 40 percent of happiness is subject to self-control.[120][121]

When discussing genetics and their effects on individuals it is important to first understand that genetics do not predict behavior. It is possible for genes to increase the likelihood of individuals being happier compared to others, but they do not 100 percent predict behavior.

At this point in scientific research, it has been hard to find a lot of evidence to support this idea that happiness is affected in some way by genetics. In a 2016 study Michael Minkov and Michael Harris Bond found that a gene by the name of SLC6A4 was not a good predictor of happiness level in humans.[122]

On the other hand, there have been many studies that have found genetics to be a key part in predicting and understanding happiness in humans. In a review article discussing many studies on genetics and happiness they discussed the common findings. The author found an important factor that has affected scientist findings this being how happiness is measured. For example, in certain studies when subjective wellbeing is measured as a trait heredity is found to be higher, about 70 to 90 percent. In another study 11,500 unrelated genotypes were studied, and the conclusion was the heritability was only 12 to 18 percent. Overall, this article found the common percent of heredity was about 20 to 50 percent.[123]

Economic and political views

Newly commissioned officers celebrate their new positions by throwing their midshipmen covers into the air as part of the U.S. Naval Academy class of 2011 graduation and commissioning ceremony.

Main article: Happiness economics

In politics, happiness as a guiding ideal is expressed in the United States Declaration of Independence of 1776, written by Thomas Jefferson, as the universal right to "the pursuit of happiness."[124] This seems to suggest a subjective interpretation but one that goes beyond emotions alone. It has to be kept in mind that the word happiness meant "prosperity, thriving, wellbeing" in the 18th century and not the same thing as it does today. In fact, happiness.[125]

Common market health measures such as GDP and GNP have been used as a measure of successful policy. On average richer nations tend to be happier than poorer nations, but this effect seems to diminish with wealth.[126][127] This has been explained by the fact that the dependency is not linear but logarithmic, i.e., the same percentual increase in the GNP produces the same increase in happiness for wealthy countries as for poor countries.[128][129][130][131] Increasingly, academic economists and international economic organizations are arguing for and developing multi-dimensional dashboards which combine subjective and objective indicators to provide a more direct and explicit assessment of human wellbeing. Work by Paul Anand and colleagues helps to highlight the fact that there many different contributors to adult wellbeing, that happiness judgement reflect, in part, the presence of salient constraints, and that fairness, autonomy, community and engagement are key aspects of happiness and wellbeing throughout the life course.[132] Although these factors play a role in happiness, they do not all need to act in simultaneously to help one achieve an increase in happiness.

Libertarian think tank Cato Institute claims that economic freedom correlates strongly with happiness[133] preferably within the context of a western mixed economy, with free press and a democracy. According to certain standards, East European countries when ruled by Communist parties were less happy than Western ones, even less happy than other equally poor countries.[134]

Since 2003, empirical research in the field of happiness economics, such as that by Benjamin Radcliff, professor of Political Science at the University of Notre Dame, supported the contention that in democratic countries life satisfaction is strongly and positively related to the social democratic model of a generous social safety net, pro-worker labor market regulations, and strong labor unions.[135][136] Similarly, there is evidence that public policies which reduce poverty and support a strong middle class, such as a higher minimum wage, strongly affect average levels of well-being.[137]

It has been argued that happiness measures could be used not as a replacement for more traditional measures, but as a supplement.[138] According to the Cato institute, people constantly make choices that decrease their happiness, because they have also more important aims. Therefore, government should not decrease the alternatives available for the citizen by patronizing them but let the citizen keep a maximal freedom of choice.[139]

Good mental health and good relationships contribute more than income to happiness and governments should take these into account.[140]

In the UK Richard Layard and others have led the development of happiness economics.

Contributing factors and research outcomes

Main article: Well-being contributing factors

Research on positive psychology, well-being, eudaimonia and happiness, and the theories of Diener, Ryff, Keyes, and Seligmann covers a broad range of levels and topics, including "the biological, personal, relational, institutional, cultural, and global dimensions of life."[141] The psychiatrist George Vaillant and the director of longitudinal Study of Adult Development at Harvard University Robert J. Waldinger found that those who were happiest and healthier reported strong interpersonal relationships.[142] Research showed that adequate sleep contributes to well-being.[143] In 2018, Laurie R. Santos course titled "Psychology and the Good Life" became the most popular course in the history of Yale University and was made

CHAPTER TWO

'Happiness'

Definitions

'Happiness' is the subject of debate on usage and meaning,[3][4][5][6][7] and on possible differences in understanding by culture.[8][9]

The word is mostly used in relation to two factors:[10]

Happy children playing in water

the current experience of the feeling of an emotion (affect) such as pleasure or joy,[1] or of a more general sense of 'emotional condition as a whole'.[11] For instance Daniel Kahneman has defined happiness as "what I experience here and now".[12] This usage is prevalent in dictionary definitions of happiness.[13][14][15]

appraisal of life satisfaction, such as of quality of life.[16] For instance Ruut Veenhoven has defined happiness as "overall appreciation of one's life as-a-whole."[17][18] Kahneman has said that this is more important to people than current experience.[19][20][21]

Some usages can include both of these factors. Subjective well-being (swb)[22] includes measures of current experience (emotions, moods, and feelings) and of life satisfaction.[nb 1] For instance Sonja Lyubomirsky has described happiness as "the experience of joy, contentment, or positive well-being, combined with a sense that one's life is good, meaningful, and worthwhile."[23] Eudaimonia,[24] is a Greek term variously translated as happiness, welfare, flourishing, and blessedness. Xavier Landes[25] has proposed that happiness include measures of subjective wellbeing, mood and eudaimonia.[26]

These differing uses can give different results.[27][28] For instance the correlation of income levels has been shown to be substantial with life satisfaction measures, but to be far weaker, at least above a certain threshold, with current experience measures.[29][30] Whereas Nordic countries often score highest on swb surveys, South American countries score higher on affect-based surveys of current positive life experiencing.[31]

The implied meaning of the word may vary depending on context,[32] qualifying happiness as a polyseme and a fuzzy concept.

A further issue is when measurement is made; appraisal of a level of happiness at the time of the experience may be different from appraisal via memory at a later date.[33][34]

Some users accept these issues, but continue to use the word because of its convening power.[35]

Philosophy

A butcher happily slicing meat

Main article: Philosophy of happiness

Relation to morality

Philosophy of happiness is often discussed in conjunction with ethics.[36] Traditional European societies, inherited from the Greeks and from Christianity, often linked happiness with morality, which was concerned with the performance in a certain kind of role in a certain kind of social life. However, with the rise of individualism, begotten partly by Protestantism and capitalism, the links between duty in a society and happiness were gradually broken. The consequence was a redefinition of the moral terms. Happiness is no longer defined in relation to social life, but in terms of individual psychology. Happiness, however, remains a difficult term for moral philosophy. Throughout the history of moral philosophy, there has been an oscillation between attempts to define morality in terms of consequences leading to happiness and attempts to define morality in terms that have nothing to do with happiness at all.[37]

Aristotle

Aristotle described eudaimonia (Greek: εὐδαιμονία) as the goal of human thought and action. Eudaimonia is often translated to mean happiness, but some scholars contend that "human flourishing" may be a more accurate translation.[38] Aristotle's use of the term in Nicomachiean Ethics extends beyond the general sense of happiness.[39]

In the Nicomachean Ethics, written in 350 BCE, Aristotle stated that happiness (also being well and doing well) is the only thing that humans desire for their own sake, unlike riches, honour, health or friendship. He observed that men sought riches, or honour, or health not only for their own sake but also in order to be happy. For Aristotle the term eudaimonia, which is translated as 'happiness' or 'flourishing' is an activity rather than an emotion or a state.[40] Eudaimonia (Greek: εὐδαιμονία) is a classical Greek word consists of the word "eu" ("good" or "well-being") and "daimōn" ("spirit" or "minor deity", used by extension to mean one's lot or fortune). Thus understood, the happy life is the good life, that is, a life in which a person fulfills human nature in an excellent way. Specifically, Aristotle argued that the good life is the life of excellent rational activity. He arrived at this claim with the "Function Argument". Basically, if it is right, every living thing has a function, that which it uniquely does. For Aristotle human function is to reason, since it is that alone which humans uniquely do. And performing one's function well, or excellently, is good. According to Aristotle, the life of excellent rational activity is the happy life. Aristotle argued a second best life for those incapable of excellent rational activity was the life of moral virtue.[41] The key question Aristotle seeks to answer is "What is the ultimate purpose of human existence?" a lot of people are seeking pleasure, health, and a good reputation. It is true that those have a value, but none of them can occupy the place of the greatest good for which humanity aims. It may seem like all goods are a means to obtain happiness, but Aristotle said that happiness is always an end in itself.

Western ethics

Western ethicists have made arguments for how humans should behave, either individually or collectively, based on the resulting happiness of such behavior. Utilitarians, such as John Stuart Mill and Jeremy Bentham, advocated the greatest happiness principle as a guide for ethical behavior.[42]

Nietzsche

Friedrich Nietzsche critiqued the English Utilitarians' focus on attaining the greatest happiness, stating that "Man does not strive for happiness, only the Englishman does." Nietzsche meant that making happiness one's ultimate goal and the aim of one's existence, in his words "makes one contemptible." Nietzsche instead yearned for a culture that would set higher, more difficult goals than "mere happiness." He introduced the quasi-dystopic figure of the "last man" as a kind of thought experiment against the utilitarians and happiness-seekers. these small, "last men" who seek after only their own pleasure and health, avoiding all danger, exertion, difficulty, challenge, struggle are meant to seem contemptible to Nietzsche's reader. Nietzsche instead wants us to consider the value of what is difficult, what can only be earned through struggle, difficulty, pain and thus to come to see the affirmative value suffering and unhappiness truly play in creating everything of great worth in life, including all the highest achievements of human culture, not least of all philosophy.[43][44]

Changes in focus over time

In 2004 Darrin McMahon claimed, that over time the emphasis shifted from the happiness of virtue to the virtue of happiness.[45]

Culture

Personal happiness aims can be effected by cultural factors.[46][47][48] Hedonism appears to be more strongly related to happiness in more individualistic cultures.[49]

A happy, youthful male

Cultural views on happiness have changed over time.[50] For instance Western concern about childhood being a time of happiness has occurred only since the 19th century.[51]

Not all cultures seek to maximise happiness,[52][nb 2][nb 3] and some cultures are averse to happiness.[53][54]

Religion

See also: Religious studies

People in countries with high cultural religiosity tend to relate their life satisfaction less to their emotional experiences than people in more secular countries.[55]

Eastern

Buddhism

Tibetan Buddhist monk

Happiness forms a central theme of Buddhist teachings.[56] For ultimate freedom from suffering, the Noble Eightfold Path leads its practitioner to Nirvana, a state of everlasting peace. Ultimate happiness is only achieved by overcoming craving in all forms. More mundane forms of happiness, such as acquiring wealth and maintaining good friendships, are also recognized as worthy goals for lay people (see sukha). Buddhism also encourages the generation of loving kindness and compassion, the desire for the happiness and welfare of all beings.[57][58][unreliable source?][unreliable source?]

Hinduism

In Advaita Vedanta, the ultimate goal of life is happiness, in the sense that duality between Atman and Brahman is transcended and one realizes oneself to be the Self in all.

Patanjali, author of the Yoga Sutras, wrote quite exhaustively on the psychological and ontological roots of bliss.[59]

Confucianism

The Chinese Confucian thinker Mencius, who had sought to give advice to ruthless political leaders during China's Warring States period, was convinced that the mind played a mediating role between the "lesser self" (the physiological self) and the "greater self" (the moral self), and that getting the priorities right between these two would lead to sage-hood. He argued that if one did not feel satisfaction or pleasure in nourishing one's "vital force" with "righteous deeds", then that force would shrivel up (Mencius, 6A:15 2A:2). More specifically, he mentions the experience of intoxicating joy if one celebrates the practice of the great virtues, especially through music.[60]

Abrahamic

Judaism

Main article: Happiness in Judaism

Happiness or simcha (Hebrew: שמחה) in Judaism is considered an important element in the service of God.[61] The biblical verse "worship The Lord with gladness; come before him with joyful songs," (Psalm 100:2) stresses joy in the service of God.[citation needed] A popular teaching by Rabbi Nachman of Breslov, a 19th-century Chassidic Rabbi, is "Mitzvah Gedolah Le'hiyot Besimcha Tamid," it is a great mitzvah (commandment) to always be in a state of happiness. When a person is happy they are much more capable of serving God and going about their daily activities than when depressed or upset.[62][self-published source?]

Roman Catholicism

The primary meaning of "happiness" in various European languages involves good fortune, chance or happening. The meaning in Greek philosophy, however, refers primarily to ethics.

In Catholicism, the ultimate end of human existence consists in felicity, Latin equivalent to the Greek eudaimonia, or "blessed happiness", described by the 13th-century philosopher-theologian Thomas Aquinas as a Beatific Vision of God's essence in the next life.[63]

According to St. Augustine and Thomas Aquinas, man's last end is happiness: "all men agree in desiring the last end, which is happiness."[64] However, where utilitarians focused on reasoning about consequences as the primary tool for reaching happiness, Aquinas agreed with Aristotle that happiness cannot be reached solely through reasoning about consequences of acts, but also requires a pursuit of good causes for acts, such as habits according to virtue.[65] In turn, which habits and acts that normally lead to happiness is according to Aquinas caused by laws: natural law and divine law. These laws, in turn, were according to Aquinas caused by a first cause, or God.[citation needed]

According to Aquinas, happiness consists in an "operation of the speculative intellect": "Consequently happiness consists principally in such an operation, viz. in the contemplation of Divine things." And, "the last end cannot consist in the active life, which pertains to the practical intellect." So: "Therefore the last and perfect happiness, which we await in the life to come, consists entirely in contemplation. But imperfect happiness, such as can be had here, consists first and principally in contemplation, but secondarily, in an operation of the practical intellect directing human actions and passions."[66]

Human complexities, like reason and cognition, can produce well-being or happiness, but such form is limited and transitory. In temporal life, the contemplation of God, the infinitely Beautiful, is the supreme delight of the will. Beatitudo, or perfect happiness, as complete well-being, is to be attained not in this life, but the next.[67]

Islam

Al-Ghazali (1058–1111), the Muslim Sufi thinker, wrote "The Alchemy of Happiness", a manual of spiritual instruction throughout the Muslim world and widely practiced today.[citation needed]

Achievement methods

Theories on how to achieve happiness include "encountering unexpected positive events",[68] "seeing a significant other",[69] and "basking in the acceptance and praise of others".[70] However others believe that happiness is not solely derived from external, momentary pleasures.[71]

Self-fulfilment theories

Woman kissing a baby on the cheek

Maslow's hierarchy of needs

Maslow's hierarchy of needs is a pyramid depicting the levels of human needs, psychological, and physical. When a human being ascends the steps of the pyramid, self-actualization is reached. Beyond the routine of needs fulfillment, Maslow envisioned moments of extraordinary experience, known as peak experiences, profound moments of love, understanding, happiness, or rapture, during which a person feels more whole, alive, self-sufficient, and yet a part of the world. This is similar to the flow concept of Mihály Csíkszentmihályi.[72] The concept of flow is the idea that after our basic needs are met we can achieve greater happiness by altering our consciousness by becoming so engaged in a task that we lose our sense of time. Our intense focus causes us to forget any other issues, which in return promotes positive emotions.

Erich Fromm

Fromm said "Happiness is the indication that man has found the answer to the problem of human existence: the productive realization of his potentialities and thus, simultaneously, being one with the world and preserving the integrity of his self. In spending his energy productively he increases his powers, he „burns without being consumed.""[73]

Self-determination theory

Smiling woman from Vietnam

Self-determination theory relates intrinsic motivation to three needs: competence, autonomy, and relatedness.

Modernization and freedom of choice

Ronald Inglehart has traced cross-national differences in the level of happiness based on data from the World Values Survey.[74] He finds that the extent to which a society allows free choice has a major impact on happiness. When basic needs are satisfied, the degree of happiness depends on economic and cultural factors that enable free choice in how people live their lives. Happiness also depends on religion in countries where free choice is constrained.[75]

Positive psychology

Since 2000 the field of positive psychology has expanded drastically in terms of scientific publications, and has produced many different views on causes of happiness, and on factors that correlate with happiness.[76] Numerous short-term self-help interventions have been developed and demonstrated to improve happiness.[77][78]

Indirect approaches

Various writers, including Camus and Tolle, have written that the act of searching or seeking for happiness is incompatible with being happy.[79][80][81][82]

John Stuart Mill believed that for the great majority of people happiness is best achieved en passant, rather than striving for it directly. This meant no self-consciousness, scrutiny, self-interrogation, dwelling on, thinking about, imagining or questioning on one's happiness. Then, if otherwise fortunately circumstanced, one would "inhale happiness with the air you breathe."[83]

Natural occurrence

William Inge observed that "on the whole, the happiest people seem to be those who have no particular cause for being happy except the fact that they are so."[84] Orison

Swett Marden said that "some people are born happy."[85]

Negative effects

June Gruber argued that happiness may have negative effects. It may trigger a person to be more sensitive, more gullible, less successful, and more likely to undertake high risk behaviours.[86] She also conducted studies suggesting that seeking happiness can have negative effects, such as failure to meet over-high expectations.[87][88][89] Iris Mauss has shown that the more people strive for happiness, the more likely they will set up too high of standards and feel disappointed.[90][91]

Limits

The idea of motivational hedonism is the theory that pleasure is the aim for human life.[92] However, according to impact bias, people are poor predictors of their future emotions.[93] Therefore, can happiness be sought after and pain be avoided, if it is considered to be unpredictable and unsustainable? Sigmund Freud said that all humans strive after happiness, but that the possibilities of achieving it are restricted because we "are so made that we can derive intense enjoyment only from a contrast and very little from the state of things."[94]

Pursuit

Not all cultures seek to maximise happiness. It has been found in Western cultures that individual happiness is the most important. However, other cultures have opposite views and tend to be aversive to the idea of individual happiness. For example, people living in Eastern Asian cultures focus more on the need for happiness within relationships with others and even find personal happiness to be harmful to fulfilling happy social relationships.[53][95][96][nb 2][nb 3]

A 2012 study found that psychological well-being was higher for people who experienced both positive and negative emotions.[97][98][99]

Examination

Happiness can be examined in experiential and evaluative contexts. Experiential well-being, or "objective happiness", is happiness measured in the moment via questions such as "How good or bad is your experience now?". In contrast, evaluative well-being asks questions such as "How good was your vacation?" and measures one's subjective thoughts and feelings about happiness in the past. Experiential well-being is less prone to errors in reconstructive memory, but the majority of literature on happiness refers to evaluative well-being. The two measures of happiness can be related by heuristics such as the peak–end rule.[100]

Some commentators focus on the difference between the hedonistic tradition of seeking pleasant and avoiding unpleasant experiences, and the eudaimonic tradition of living life in a full and deeply satisfying way.[101]

Measurement

People have been trying to measure happiness for centuries. In 1780, the English utilitarian philosopher Jeremy Bentham proposed that as happiness was the primary goal of humans it should be measured as a way of determining how well the government was performing.[102]

Several scales have been developed to measure happiness:

The Subjective Happiness Scale (SHS) is a four-item scale, measuring global subjective happiness from 1999. The scale requires participants to use absolute ratings to characterize themselves as happy or unhappy individuals, as well as it asks to what extent they identify themselves with descriptions of happy and unhappy individuals.[103][104]

The Positive and Negative Affect Schedule (PANAS) from 1988 is a 20-item questionnaire, using a five-point Likert scale (1 = very slightly or not at all, 5 = extremely) to assess the relation between personality traits and positive or negative affects at "this moment, today, the past few days, the past week, the past few weeks, the past year, and in general".[105] A longer version with additional affect scales was published 1994.[106]

The Satisfaction with Life Scale (SWLS) is a global cognitive assessment of life satisfaction developed by Ed Diener. A seven-point Likert scale is used to agree or disagree with five statements about one's life.[107][108]

The Cantril ladder method[109] has been used in the World Happiness Report. Respondents are asked to think of a ladder, with the best possible life for them being a 10, and the worst possible life being a 0. They are then asked to rate their own current lives on that 0 to 10 scale.[110][109]

Positive Experience; the survey by Gallup asks if, the day before, people experienced enjoyment, laughing or smiling a lot, feeling well-rested, being treated with respect, learning or doing something interesting. 9 of the top 10 countries in 2018 were South American, led by Paraguay and Panama. Country scores range from 85 to 43.[1

CHAPTER THREE

A longer version

Several terms redirect here. For other uses, see Happiness (disambiguation), Happy (disambiguation), Gladness (disambiguation) and Jolly (disambiguation).

"Enjoyment" redirects here. For the 2005 video album by Kaiser Chiefs, see Enjoyment (video).

"Cheerful" redirects here. For Royal Navy destroyer, see HMS Cheerful (1897).

A smiling 95-year-old man from Pichilemu, Chile

Part of a series on

Emotions

Affect

Classification

In animals

Emotional intelligence

Mood

Regulation

Interpersonal

Dysregulation

Valence

Emotions

v

t

e

The term happiness is used in the context of mental or emotional states, including positive or pleasant emotions ranging from contentment to intense joy.[1] It is also used in the context of life satisfaction, subjective well-being, eudaimonia, flourishing and well-being.[2]

Since the 1960s, happiness research has been conducted in a wide variety of scientific disciplines, including gerontology, social psychology and positive psychology, clinical and medical research and happiness economics.